Me Nan
found a
Leprechaun

written by David McNiven
illustrated by Margaret Anne Suggs

To: _____

From: _____

First edition 2014

Written, illustrated, designed, produced and printed entirely in Ireland.
Printed by Donegan Print, Wexford
ISBN 978-0-9931688-0-2

Me Nan has found a Leprechaun
sure he's been with her for a week.

She found him on a fairy mound,

ye should come an' have a peek.

He's got these funny pointy ears
an' a great big woolly hat,
an' loves to ride around the place
on Nan's auld fluffy cat.

He likes a glass o' Guinness
an' boiled cabbage with the ham,
his spuds with melted butter
an' the soda bread with jam.

He'll say "top o' the mornin'"
or, "begor, 'tis well ye look,"
an', "well how ye goin' on now
sure I hope ye likes this book!"

She found him on a country walk
poor lad was frozen cold.
He was sittin' in the pourin' rain
on his little pot o' gold

He says to her, "oim Moicháel
but sure you can call me Mick.
I've me little pot o' gold here
ain't you welcome to a pick!

"Now missus would ye help me up
Sure me bum is frozen cold
sat at the end of this here rainbow
on me little pot o' gold!"

Says he, "ye wouldn't have aer a sandwich
or a nice big lump o' cake
sure me belly thinks me throat's cut
I haven't eaten for a wake!"

Says Nan, "Sure you could make a wish?"
"Well begor," says he, "tis true
but sure I cannot wish it for meself
but I'll make any wish for you"

Says Nan, "I'll wish a slice of cake,
a sandwich and some tae
an' to be sure that you're not messin'
sure we'll have it right away"

Says he, "missus yer the best o' sorts
sure what more can I say
I'll wish a nice big lump o' cake
an some whiskey an' the tae"

An' there it was before her
on a tree stump, just like that!

A bowl of steaming porridge . . .

. . . an' some custard in a hat?!!

Says he, "there's a surprise now!!
Gor I never wished for that
but sure if you would eat the custard
I could be doin' with the hat".

"D'you have a nice warm car," says he,
"sure we're frozen, both of us."
"The only wheels I use," says Nan, "are on Thursday's bingo bus."

"A car!" says she, "begor I wish,"
says he, "what colour would ye like?"
"Oh red," says Nan…but it's emerald green…

...it's a great big motor bike!

Jayney you should see me Nan now,
be the Lord lads what a fright!
Goggles, helmet an' black leathers
as she roars off out of sight.

An' Mick's there in da goggles
with his little face all smiles
sure he sits there on Nan's shoulders
as they're burning up de miles.

An she's roarin' down the back lanes
with her red scarf flyin' out
an' the neighbours yells, "bejaysus
lads there's hooligans about!"

Nan says that he's a lovely lad
but he's not right in the head
no matter what he wishes for
he gets somethin' else instead.

Sure he's always doin' magic
an' it's always going wrong.
Says he, "your doorbell's banjaxed."
She has this man now with a gong!???"

Sure she couldn't do her washin',
her machine had sprung a lake,
but somehow he wished a telly.
She's no clothes washed for a wake!

An' he said he'd fix her kettle,
sure he fixed it right away.
Says she, 'I've got this blender thing
that makes ne'er a drop o' tae.'

He saw her little garden seat
the frames was broke an' bent.
Says he, "loungers an' a parasol,"

but sure now she's got a tent.

"I'd like a mobile phone," says she,
"sure wouldn't that be jolly."
So Mick got her an auld phone box
that's in a shopping trolley!

When Aunty Bridie came, says she,
"I wish I'd a lad like that."
Mick says, "I'll get de brudder."

Now she's got a ginger cat!

There's worse to come, the priest says,
"well begor I likes the bike!"
So Mick he says, "I'll make the wish,"
an' sure he gets a kiddie's trike!

Now there's some folks cannot see him
an' they think me Nan is cracked
sure Nan never stops the talkin'
an' Mick's there, he's talkin' back.

Sure he doesn't just do magic
he can make things disappear
or he'll maybe find a golden coin
right there behind yer ear.

One day he lost the table
an' the dresser an' six chairs.

When Nan went up to bed that night . . .

. . . she found 'em all up stairs.

Me da says, "they're the perfect pair
it's right clear for all to see.
The whole world knows yer Nan is cracked
an' yer man he's is off his tree."

But Nan says she's gonna keep him
don't be thinkin' she's gone soft
sure she's got his little pot o' gold
an' they keeps it in the loft!